Puzzle of the Pyramid

Written by Ciaran Murtagh

Illustrated by Katy Riddell

Collins

Chapter 1

Auntie Flo has always been up for an adventure. For my birthday, she bought me tickets to a treetop climbing course. The birthday before that it was water-skiing lessons, and before that she wanted to go sledging with huskies. The strange thing is, she always got tickets for herself too! It's almost like my birthday was an excuse for *her* to have fun!

That's why it was no surprise when she decided to go to Egypt to explore a pyramid. It was all for charity. The whole family helped raise the sponsorship money.

We went to the coach to wave her off. She wore a big backpack and an even bigger smile! She gave me and Mum a kiss and promised she'd see us again soon.

That was the last we heard from her,
until the postcard arrived ...

Mum and I are not suspicious people, but there was something very strange about the postcard Auntie Flo sent. It just didn't sound like her.

Tanya. Big fun on the journey. Trouble with my suitcase. Here safe now. Please tell Lola hello from me. Send her my love. Help your brother in the shed at the end of the garden.

Love Auntie Flo.

Weird right?

To make sure I wasn't going mad, I went to fetch one of the other postcards Auntie Flo had sent so I could compare.

Auntie Flo always sent Mum and me postcards from her travels. We kept them on the fridge. I grabbed the one she had sent from Paris last year to see if it was any different.

Hey, Tan! Hey, Lola!
How's it going? Having a great time in Paris. There is so much to do. I went up the Eiffel Tower, saw the Mona Lisa and ate a cheese toastie – here they call it a "croque fromage" – fancy huh?!
Love ya lots! Flo!
xxxx

That postcard sounded like Auntie Flo; the other one sounded like it had been written by a robot! She never called my mum Tanya and who cared about her suitcase? And the *really* weird thing was I don't have a brother, or a shed ... we don't even have a garden!

I knew that Flo was trying to tell us something. I looked at the postcard for ages until it hit me. The first words of each sentence spelt out a message.

Tanya. Big fun on the journey. Trouble with my suitcase. Here safe now. Please tell Lola hello from me. Send her my love. Help your brother in the shed at the end of the garden.

Love Auntie Flo.

Chapter 2

When Mum saw the message, she knew I was on
to something. We packed our bags, cleared out our
savings and booked two tickets on the fastest plane
to Cairo. As we got our things together, I realised we
didn't know exactly where in Egypt Auntie Flo had
gone – it was a big place!

Mum said that Auntie Flo had emailed her the advert
when she'd first heard about the adventure, so we
scrolled through the messages on her phone, looking
for the right one.

When she found it, she passed over the phone so
I could see.

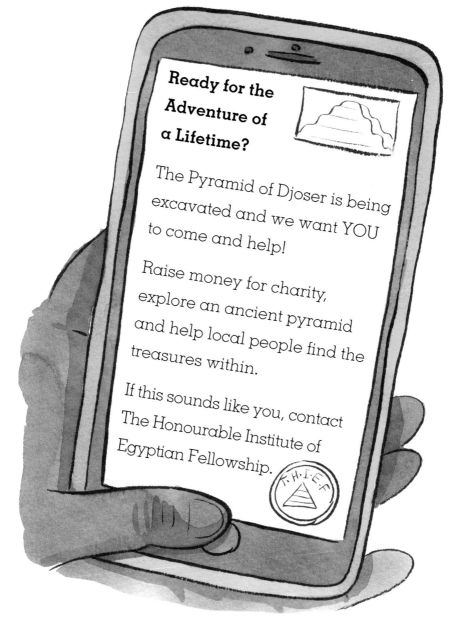

Ready for the Adventure of a Lifetime?

The Pyramid of Djoser is being excavated and we want YOU to come and help!

Raise money for charity, explore an ancient pyramid and help local people find the treasures within.

If this sounds like you, contact The Honourable Institute of Egyptian Fellowship.

There was no time to lose. Mum took the phone back and used it to call a taxi. We were going to the Pyramid of Djoser.

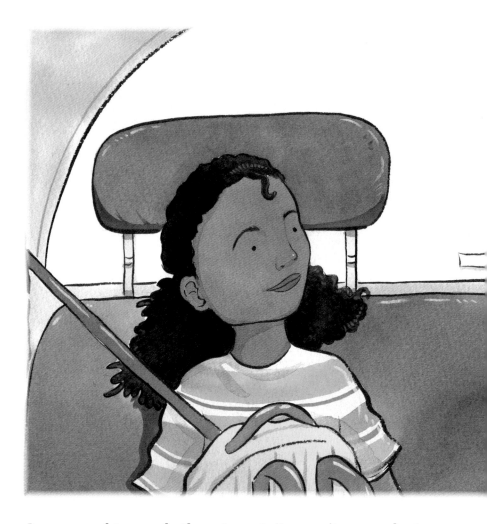

As we sped towards the airport, I wasn't sure what we were getting ourselves into, but I knew we needed to find out more. We had a long journey ahead of us so I decided to start at the beginning.

Auntie Flo's trip to Egypt had got a lot of attention.

The local newspaper had even sent a reporter to
interview her on the day she left. I'd kept the cutting
in my diary. As we sat in the back of the taxi,
I pulled it out of my bag and began to read,
searching for clues.

Local adventurer Flo Sampson, 52, is off
on her travels again. Having visited Peru,
India and Madagascar in recent years,
Flo is now all set for her latest adventure.

"I'm off to an Egyptian pyramid,"
she gushed. "I can't wait to get there.
I'm part of a team looking for treasure."

Flo is travelling with a group of 11
like-minded people and will spend two
weeks working in the desert outside Cairo.

The expedition is to raise funds for The Honourable Institute of Egyptian Fellowship. The head of the organisation, Rupert Raab, dressed for success in a crisp linen suit, is sure the trip will be great.

"If everything goes to plan, this will be one for the history books!" he said.

Flo can't wait to get to work.

"I love adventure and I love helping people," she said. "This is the perfect trip for me!"

Chapter 3

When we arrived at
the airport, we rushed
through the security
gates to the plane.
While we waited in
the departure lounge, I told
Mum what I had learnt.

"We need to find
Rupert Raab," she said.
"If anyone knows what's
happened to my sister,
it's him. Was there a picture
of him in the paper?"

I shook my head and
showed Mum the cutting.
No picture of Rupert, just
a big picture of Auntie Flo,
grinning before she
clambered on to a coach.
She seemed so happy,
I hoped she was all right.

Mum sensed what I was thinking. She gave my shoulder a squeeze.

"Don't worry, love," she said. "Auntie Flo's been in some sticky situations before. I remember, once, on her blog, she wrote about fighting off a poisonous spider in the Amazon with a pair of sunglasses. That's your Auntie Flo, she's always got something up her sleeve."

But I had stopped listening. Auntie Flo's blog –
of course! She uploaded something nearly every day.
Maybe that would help us get to the bottom of this.

I asked if I could borrow Mum's phone. If I was quick,
I could read the latest upload before we boarded
the plane.

Wotcha adventurers! Fearless Flo here, just landed in Egypt and I'm about to check into my hotel, The Pharaoh's Rest. Not that I'll be seeing much of it! I'm not here to rest – I'm here to work! We'll be up at the crack of dawn and heading into the pyramid. I'll keep you posted!

Only she hadn't kept us posted at all because that had been her last entry. Just then, they called us on to the plane. Now I knew where we were heading when we landed. We were going to start the search for Auntie Flo at The Pharaoh's Rest.

When we landed in Cairo, we found a friendly taxi driver to take us straight to the hotel.

"The Pharaoh's Rest!" he said, sounding shocked. "I haven't heard that name in a long time. I thought that hotel closed down."

Mum and I exchanged a funny look.

"Closed?" said Mum. "It can't be; my sister checked in last week."

"We haven't heard from her since, apart from one really weird postcard," I added.

The taxi driver shrugged. "Maybe I got it wrong," he said. "Or maybe it opened again. We'll soon find out."

The road to the hotel was long and dusty. When we got to the hotel itself, it certainly looked like it should have closed down. The illuminated sign flickered on and off, and the paint was peeling from the walls.

"Charming," said Mum, wrinkling her nose.

The taxi driver pulled to a halt.

"You don't have to stay here," he said. "I know a nice hotel five minutes away."

I shook my head. The Pharaoh's Rest was the last place we knew my auntie had been. It was where we were going too.

Chapter 4

Inside, the hotel was dustier than outside! I walked up to the reception desk and rang the bell. A man scurried out of the gloom. He was dressed in a faded uniform and seemed surprised to see us.

"Yes?" he said. "Can I help you?"

"We're looking for my auntie," I began. "Flo Sampson."

"Never heard of her," he stuttered, licking his lips.

"Are you sure?" I said, fishing the newspaper cutting out of my bag to show him the picture. I held it up for him to see.

"Never seen her either," he said, not even looking at the photo.

"We'll take a room," said Mum. "We'll spend the night and look properly in the morning."

"I am sorry, ladies," said the receptionist, wringing his hands. "We're full."

Mum and I looked at the deserted reception and restaurant.

"Full!" snorted Mum. "Are you sure?"

Before he had chance to answer, another man strode into reception. He hadn't spotted us. He wore a dusty linen suit.

"Another successful day, Richard. Let's lock up and get out of here –"

He frowned when he saw us standing by the reception desk.

"They're looking for a room," said the receptionist.

"But of course," said the man in the linen suit. "Room five is free, I think."

The receptionist rummaged in a drawer for a key.

"I thought you were fully booked?" I said.

"No, no," said the man in the linen suit.
"One room free. Forgive my brother, he gets confused.
Let me help with your bags."

Once the man had left us in our room, I turned to Mum. We were both thinking the same thing. Was the man in the dusty linen suit Rupert Raab? If he was, why were he and his brother pretending to run a hotel?

That night I couldn't sleep. Mum was snoring like a tractor and I was thirsty.

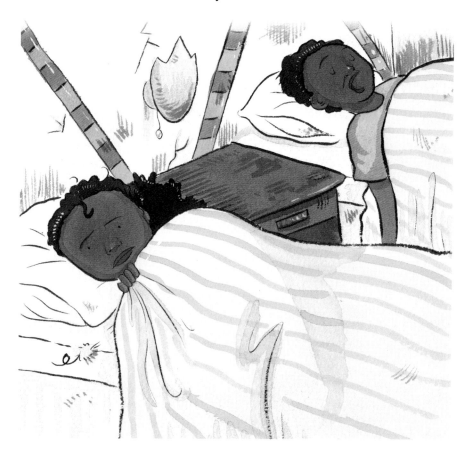

I set out to find a glass of water. As I made my way downstairs, I heard hushed voices coming from behind a door.

"Why did you let them stay?"

"I didn't! You said we had a room. I was getting rid of them."

"It doesn't matter now. We'll just have to get rid of them in the morning."

"What if they find out?"

"They won't! Trust me! Everything is going to plan. This one's for the history books."

I gasped. I'd heard those words somewhere before. I turned and ran back to my room as fast as I could.

In the room, I turned on
the bedside light and fished out
the newspaper cutting. I read
again the words that Rupert
had said to the reporter:

"If everything goes
to plan, this will be one
for the history books."

Now there was no doubt in my
mind: the man downstairs was
Rupert Raab. But if he was here,
where was my auntie and where
were the rest of the expedition?
I thought about waking Mum
and telling her everything,
but what would be the point
in that? We wouldn't be able to
do anything until the morning
and at least one of us should get
some sleep. I pulled the covers
up to my chin and lay
the pillow over my eyes.

Chapter 5

I must have fallen asleep, because when I woke, Mum was standing by the window.

"Morning, sleepyhead," she said, when she noticed I was awake. "What do you think of that then?"

She gestured to the view. The ruins of a pyramid lay just beyond the grounds of the hotel and it was bathed in golden sunlight.

"I think we're in the right place," I said, with a smile. Then I filled her in on what I had found out the night before. Now all we had to do was find Auntie Flo and the others and get out of there.

As we spoke, the receptionist emerged from the back door of the hotel. We ducked away from the window and watched. He scurried down the dusty yard and disappeared into a hut at the far end of the garden.

"I wonder where he's going in such a hurry," said Mum, and then the final clue clicked into place.

I rushed to my bag and pulled out the postcard.

"Help your brother in the shed at the end of the garden."

Suddenly it made sense! Auntie Flo was leading us right to where we needed to be. It wasn't my non-existent brother she was talking about. It was Rupert's.

"We've got to follow him," I told Mum. "He'll lead us to Flo. I'm sure of it."

We snuck out of our room, checking both ways for
signs of Rupert. He was nowhere to be seen. We crept
down the stairs and tiptoed out through the garden.
When we got to the shed, I put my ear to the door and
listened … nothing. I flung open the door.

Mum and I gasped at the sight before us.
We couldn't believe our eyes. The shed was filled
with glittering treasure. There were gold coins,
a sarcophagus and even an elaborate death mask.

"They're robbing the pyramid," I said.

"And I think I know how," said Mum, pointing to
a hole in the centre of the floor. "There's a tunnel."

Mum was about to jump down, when I stopped her.

"Give me your phone."

Mum handed it over. If we were going down a tunnel after some pyramid robbers, we were going to need back up. I dialled the numbers and asked for the police.

"Maybe we should wait for them?" said Mum.

I shook my head.

"They know we're here. They know who we're looking for. We don't have time to wait. We need to find Auntie Flo."

Mum nodded and jumped into the tunnel and I jumped after.

As we crawled out of the other end of the tunnel, we found ourselves in a spectacular cavern. We were in the heart of the pyramid. Treasure sparkled all around and in the centre were 12 bedraggled workers – one of them was Auntie Flo. Camp beds had been set up for them and they were loading treasure into a trolley.

Mum was about to call out when I stopped her. Rupert and Robert were coming to check everyone was working hard enough.

"Put your backs into it!" shouted Rupert.

We needed to do something, but what?

I picked up a rock from the dusty floor and hurled it far into the distance. It landed with a thud and Rupert and Robert turned to investigate.

I crept towards my auntie.
Her face lit up when she saw me
and Mum coming towards her.
She smothered us both in
a dusty hug.

"You got my postcard?"
she hissed. "I knew
you'd come. They're not
a charity – they're robbers!
They're treating us
like slaves."

We had to get everybody
out and I thought
I knew how.

Chapter 6

While Robert and Rupert investigated the sound, we led the workers to the tunnel. Mum went first, leading the way, and one by one, the tired and dusty men and women followed. I stayed behind with Auntie Flo to keep watch for the brothers.

Once the last person had gone, I turned to Auntie Flo.

"Now you," I said.

Auntie Flo shook her head. "You first."

I shook my head right back.

"You're tired and weak. If the brothers come back, you'll never get away. I might just stand a chance."

Auntie Flo nodded and clambered into the tunnel.

Just as I was about to turn and follow,
the brothers returned and found the
cavern empty.

"Where's everybody gone?" spluttered Rupert.

"They must have escaped!" shouted Robert.

They looked towards the tunnel entrance.
I darted behind a rock, but it was too late.
They had seen me.

"You!" snarled Rupert. "After her!"

They ran towards me. I needed to think fast.
I looked at the trolley loaded with treasure.
I ran over and tipped the treasure on to
the floor. Then I ran towards the tunnel,
pushing the trolley in front of me. At the
last moment, I hopped into it and rode it
like a go-kart through the darkness.

I could hear Rupert and Robert racing
after me. Good. If the rest of my scheme
was going to plan, that was exactly what
I wanted them to do.

I emerged at the bottom of the hole and Mum and Flo pulled me to safety. Rupert and Robert crawled out after, right into the waiting arms of the police.

They tried to explain, but the evidence was there for all to see. They were using volunteers to rob a pyramid, with a disused hotel as a cover story.

When we got home, the reporters were there for an interview.

"I didn't do it all by myself," she said. "My mum and the local police did a great job too."

Lola is the niece of local adventurer, Flo Sampson. It was her postcard that alerted Lola and her Mum to the crime.

Hero Lola Sampson, ten, uncovered a mystery, saved her aunt and returned looted Egyptian treasure all in one day.

"I always thought I was the only adventurous one in the family," Flo said. "Turns out I was wrong!"

Blog-a-Lola

I've taken a leaf out of my auntie's book – or should that be webpage out of her blog!? – and stepped into the blogosphere! Turns out this wasn't the first time those bad guys had been bad guys, and now they're both behind bars. The looted treasure was put into a museum with a display all about me, Mum and my auntie – how cool is that?

My family are famous!
Auntie Flo has promised to take
me with her on her next adventure
in the school holidays, so check
back here to find out where we're
going next! You could also check
my auntie's blog, I guess, but
my blog is way cooler :-)
Just kidding, Auntie Flo! See you
all next time!

Ideas for reading

Written by Christine Whitney

Primary Literacy Consultant

Reading objectives:
- discuss the sequence of events in books
- make inferences on the basis of what is being said and done
- predict what might happen on the basis of what has been read so far
- discuss and clarify the meanings of words, linking new meanings to known vocabulary

Spoken language objectives:
- ask relevant questions to extend understanding and knowledge

- use spoken language to develop understanding through speculating, hypothesising, imagining and exploring ideas
- participate in discussions

Curriculum links: History

Word count: 3004

Interest words: pyramid, expedition, excavated, sarcophagus

Resources: paper and pencils

Build a context for reading

- Ask children to discuss with one another what they already know about ancient Egypt and the pyramids. Check children's understanding of the word *pyramid*.

- Look at the front cover and ask children to list and then discuss what they can see in the artwork. What does the front cover suggest the story will be about?

- Read the blurb together. Ask children what further information they now have about the story and to add this to their initial predictions. Challenge them to summarise their prediction about what will happen in the story.

Understand and apply reading strategies

- Read Chapter 1. Ask children to summarise what they know about Auntie Flo by the end of this chapter.